Avocado Avenue

Pilliard Dickle

First Printing, 2015

ISBN 978-0-9889568-4-1

This is a work of fiction. Any resemblance to actual persons is purely coincidental. Except for Rodney. The author did know a guy kind of like Rodney.

Printed on non-acid-free paper. In other words, the paper is loaded with acid. Particularly page 56.

Boll Weevil Press
Newnan GA

www.PilliardDickle.com

Please do not lick page 56.

Failing to fetch me at first, keep encouraged,

Missing me one place, search another,

I stop somewhere waiting for you.

Walt Whitman

Avocado Avenue

Part 1

A Gazebo in the Middle of Nowhere

Looking Out Across the Lawn

Looking out across the lawn in the late afternoon, everything is cool and quiet, except for the chattering of sparrows in the oaks overhead and the gentle wooden rumblings of the rocking chairs as they rock back and forth across the floor of the front porch.

A Gazebo in the Middle of Nowhere

"A gazebo in the middle of nowhere," said Rodney all of a sudden, looking up from his notebook.

Sally turned toward him from across the porch.

The old man didn't seem to notice, he just kept on rocking.

Rocking

"What did you say?" said Sally.

"A gazebo in the middle of nowhere," Rodney repeated, rocking back and forth in his big white wooden rocking chair, just like the old man's.

Sally looked at him for a moment, slightly bewildered.

" 'A gazebo in the middle of nowhere'?" she echoed.

Rodney nodded.

" " "A gazebo in the middle of nowhere,' " ' he said again, quoting her quoting him.

This confirmed that this was indeed what Sally thought she'd heard him say, but she still had no idea what to do with these words. So, slowly and deliberately, she quoted what Rodney had said, yet again.

" " " 'A gazebo...in the middle...of nowhere.' " ' "

By now the old man had taken notice of all this. His head was turning slightly back and forth—to the left, to the right, to the left, to the right—as Sally and Rodney said "a gazebo in the middle of nowhere" to each other across the porch for no apparent reason.

The Two Eccentric Sisters

The two eccentric sisters were out for a stroll. They came out of the mansion every Sunday afternoon. Nobody knew what they did in there all week, but every Sunday afternoon they'd go out walking and appear to act perfectly normal.

Around the corner they came, sauntering down the sidewalk as if they were not eccentric at all.

Doris and Delores

"Here come those two eccentric sisters," said the old man.

The two eccentric sisters opened the little wooden gate and walked down the brick walkway that lead to the front porch. The old man threw his hand up, and so did Sally. And so did the two eccentric sisters.

Their names were Doris and Delores, but no one ever called them that, they just called them "the two eccentric sisters," as if they were one person and that was their collective name.

"Hi," said Sally.

"Hi," said one of the two eccentric sisters, with a slight nod of the head.

She always did that. Whenever Sally said hi to her, she would always say hi back and nod her head slightly. She was predictable that way.

Ping Pong

The two eccentric sisters, Doris and Delores, sat down on the porch swing and started slowly swinging. Every now and then one of them would glance at the old man. They had noticed when they were walking down the sidewalk that his head had been wavering back and forth, to the left and to the right, as if he were watching a ping pong match. They were curious whether this might be the beginning of a tic or some sort of spasmodic affectation.

So as they sat and swung, they cast occasional glances his way. They were discreet about it, though, acting as if they were glancing at various objects in his proximity, such as the begonias or the wooden shutters, to ensure he wouldn't notice they were monitoring his head.

The old man found this insufferably annoying. In fact, he was beginning to wonder if the two eccentric sisters, who were not known for gratuitously moving their heads around, were developing some sort of a movement disorder.

What's Rodney Doing Now?

After a couple of minutes of clandestine head monitoring, yielding nothing, one of the two eccentric sisters broke the silence.

"What's Rodney doing now?" she said to Sally.

This was the usual question she asked Sally on Sunday afternoons.

"He's saying 'a gazebo in the middle of nowhere,' over and over," said Sally.

"Why is he doing that?" asked the same eccentric sister.

"I haven't the faintest idea," replied Sally.

Nobody said anything else for a moment or two, they just swung and rocked. Everybody was waiting to see if the two eccentric sisters were going to do anything eccentric.

But they didn't.

They never did.

That's what was so amazing.

Well? Is Rodney Going to Say It?

The two eccentric sisters were waiting, too. They were waiting to see if Rodney was going to say, "a gazebo in the middle of nowhere" again.

They had never actually heard him say it, they'd only heard Sally say he'd said it. But they wanted to hear Rodney say it.

It wasn't as if they didn't believe Sally—they were perfectly satisfied that Rodney had said it. Sally's word was good enough.

But: what else was there to do on a Sunday afternoon on Avocado Avenue but sit and see if Rodney was going to say "a gazebo in the middle of nowhere" again, for no apparent reason?

No, He's Not

But Rodney never said it. He Just kept on writing in his notebook.

And Sally kept on sitting in her big white rocking chair, with her feet propped up on the banister, waiting for the two eccentric sisters to do something eccentric. She was thinking: This might be the day.

And the old man just kept on rocking.

All This Time the Old Man

All this time the old man had never said a word to the two eccentric sisters. He'd thrown his hand up as they sauntered up the walkway toward the porch—as had Sally and Rodney—but he'd not actually spoken to them.

And there was a good reason, too. All he could think of to say was, "What the hell have you two been doing cooped up in that mansion all week?"

He thought it best not to say this. So he kept his mouth shut.

Canon for Porch Swing, Sparrows And Rocking Chairs

The two eccentric sisters had added a new sound to the symphony of noises: the creaking of the porch swing chains.

The porch swing creaking, the rocking chairs rumbling and the sparrows chattering in the oaks. Those were the only sounds on this quiet Sunday afternoon on Avocado Avenue.

Rodney's Notebook

Everybody wondered why Rodney had said, "a gazebo in the middle of nowhere," but nobody had actually asked Rodney. He did have a reason, though. And if anyone had bothered to ask, or had taken a look at what he was writing, they'd have known the answer.

It was all right there in his Blue Horse notebook.

Finally, Something Happened

It was beginning to look like Rodney was not going to say "a gazebo in the middle of nowhere" again, and that the two eccentric sisters were not going to do anything eccentric.

After all, they never had. So why should they start now?

Suddenly one of the two eccentric sisters gently nudged her sibling and canted her eyes toward the old man. His head was turning slightly to the left, then to the right. He had also pursed his lips and was emitting a small jet of air.

That nailed it. This was definitely the start of something pathological. They were sure.

But it wasn't. He was simply shaking his head in annoyance, and letting out an exasperated sigh.

Finally he stood up. He just couldn't take it any more.

"I'm going in the house," he announced.

Then the old man turned and went into the house.

Why Did he Go in the House?

The two eccentric sisters assumed the old man had gone in the house to use the bathroom. He had to use it a lot, they'd noticed. Every time they stopped by, it wasn't five minutes before the old man stood up and went in the house to use the bathroom.

But none of this was true. Rodney and Sally knew the real reason the old man went in the house so much: to seek refuge from the two eccentric sisters. He couldn't stand them.

In the Parlor

Now the old man was sitting in the parlor in the back of the house, overlooking the garden. In the middle of the garden, among the lush greenery, and at the end of a little walkway of stepping stones, was a gazebo.

The old man wondered if that was the gazebo Rodney wants talking about.

Probably not, he figured. Rodney had said, "a gazebo in the middle of nowhere," and that gazebo was not in the middle of nowhere. It was in the backyard.

Francine's Tastebud Transplant

While the old man was gazing at the gazebo, Sally and the two eccentric sisters were on the tail end of a conversation about a neighbor's recent tastebud transplant.

"So, I wonder if the person who had the taste buds before they were transplanted onto Francine's tongue tasted things any differently than Francine?" Sally was saying.

"Hmmm. Maybe she'll start liking asparagus again," said one of the eccentric sisters—the same one who had asked why Rodney had kept saying "a gazebo in the middle of nowhere." (Nobody knew which eccentric sister was Doris and which was Dolores.)

"Maybe she will," said Sally. "I guess we'll just have to wait and see what happens when she gets her bandages off."

Luckily, the old man was sitting safely inside the parlor, where he couldn't hear any of this.

Would J'all Like Some Tea?

There was not much more to be said about Francine's taste buds beyond what had already been said, so everybody just sat quietly for a few moments, enjoying the symphony of Sunday afternoon noises. Except for Rodney, who was busy writing in his notebook.

"Would j'all like some tea?" said Sally after a while.

"Thank you, no," said the same eccentric sister who had wondered whether Francine would start liking asparagus again. "We just had a cup of Ovaltine before we left the house."

Sally thought this was odd. The two eccentric sisters hardly ever drank Ovaltine—only on very special occasions. Everyone knew this. The eccentric sisters were very adamant about it. But no special occasion had occurred lately. At least none that Sally knew of.

Then that same eccentric sister changed her mind:

"On second thought, we are rather thirsty. Tea would

be lovely."

It seems that this eccentric sister was the spokeswoman for both the eccentric sisters. She was their collective voice. Nobody could remember the other eccentric sister's ever having said anything, or being consulted for her opinion about anything.

Sally Got Up

Sally got up and went into the house to get the two eccentric sister some tea. Now Rodney was alone on the porch with the two eccentric sisters.

Second Movement, Pianissimo

Now that Sally and of the old man were in the house, there was only the sound of one rocking chair rocking. The creaking of the porch swing chains had ceased, too. The eccentric sister who had decided they'd like some tea had now decided she was tired of swinging, so the two eccentric sisters has stopped swinging and were just sitting silently in the swing, looking out across the lawn and listening.

The sparrows were still chattering in the oaks, but they had moved down the block, congregating now in more distant branches, so that their chattering was further away. The only noticeable noise was the faint sound of a faraway freight train, fading away.

So the second movement of the symphony of Sunday afternoon noises was a quiet one. Pianissimo, as they say.

Suddenly Rodney

Suddenly Rodney stopped rocking and looked up from his notebook. The two eccentric sisters turned toward him. They thought he was about to say "a gazebo in the middle of nowhere" again.

In fact, they were positive.

You could almost hear them holding their collective breaths.

But it never happened. Rodney had looked up because he thought maybe the two eccentric sisters were about to do something eccentric.

Trying to Think of Something to Say

Rodney sat there looking at the two eccentric sisters, and the two eccentric sisters set there looking at Rodney.

Rodney felt as though he should say something, to break the awkward silence.

He had no idea his saying "a gazebo in the middle of nowhere" was such a source of amusement to the two eccentric sisters. Otherwise, he'd have been glad to say it. It would have done just fine.

Something about Francine would have sufficed as well. Not as well as "a gazebo in the middle of nowhere," but at least it would have demonstrated that Rodney had been paying attention to the conversation. But the truth was, he hadn't heard one word about Francine.

So Rodney just sat and look at the two eccentric sisters, trying to think of something to say.

Rodney Opened His Mouth

After ten long seconds, Rodney open his mouth.

The two eccentric sisters leaned forward. Their hearts skipped a beat.

This was it.

They could already hear the word "A" coming out of his mouth. One of the eccentric sisters—the one who never said anything—even thought she heard part of the word "gazebo."

Unbearable Silence

Somebody had to say something. It was imperative. The silence was becoming unbearable. It was growing louder than the chattering of the sparrows down the street. It was becoming so loud that Rodney was afraid the neighbors would start coming out of their houses to find out what was going on. Rodney spotted Mrs. Whitmore across the street peering out her front door to see what the hell was happening.

It was obvious that the two eccentric sisters had no intention of saying anything. It was up to Rodney.

Nurkle

One of the things Rodney thought about saying was "nurkle." It didn't mean anything in particular that he knew of, it just flashed through his mind for lack of anything else.

So while the two eccentric sisters anxiously awaited "a gazebo in the middle of nowhere" to emerge from Rodney's mouth, Rodney was considering saying the word "nurkle" just to see how they would react.

He could picture it now: Sally coming back onto the porch with the tea, and one of the eccentric sisters (not the one who never says anything, but the other one) announcing that Rodney had said nurkle.

Or who knows, it might have incited the other eccentric sister to say something.

"Rodney said 'nurkle,'" he could imagine her chortling.

Then Sally would probably have gone back into the parlor and told the old man, "Guess what? The eccentric sister who never says anything just said something!"

"What did she say'?" the old man would have said.

"She said, 'Rodney said "nurkle!'"

Etc. etc.

This nonsensical train of thought flashed through Rodney's mind as he searched for something that could be said to the two eccentric sisters, who were leaning forward.

Bullets

Finally, Rodney did say something to the two eccentric sisters. It wasn't "a gazebo in the middle of nowhere," though, like they had hoped it would be. It wasn't "nurkle" either.

"Would you like to hear some of my novel?" said Rodney.

His words shattered the silence like bullets shattering glass.

Mrs. Whitmore turned and went back inside.

Life was back to normal on Avocado Avenue.

Disappointed

Needless to say, the two eccentric sisters were disappointed that Rodney had not said "a gazebo in the middle of nowhere," but they tried not to show it.

"Oh, you're writing a novel?" said the eccentric sister who spoke for both the eccentric sisters, to keep from what she really wanted to say, which was "No."

Rodney took "Oh, you're writing a novel" to mean that they did want to hear some of it. Otherwise, why would they have shown such interest?

So, Rodney began reading from his novel.

Rodney's Novel

Rodney's book was constructed like a sandwich. A story-within-a-story. The meat of the novel was moderately tolerable, but the two slices of bread it was sandwiched between meandered aimlessly like a chicken in a hedgemaze. (This was by design, a sort of litmus test to cull out his true fans.) Unfortunately, it was the bread part he decided to read from.

But what choice did the two eccentric sisters have, Rodney figured, except to sit there and listen? After all, Sally was in the house getting them tea—they certainly weren't going to get up and walk away before she came back. And finishing off two huge tumblers of tea would take another twenty minutes or so, especially for the two eccentric sisters, who were slow drinkers.

"Yeah, those teas'll tie 'em down," thought Rodney, grinning smugly to himself as he flipped back to the first page in his notebook and started reading.

Bobbing

As Rodney read from his terrible novel, the two eccentric sisters nodded their heads occasionally, as if they were listening attentively. But they weren't. They were simply bobbing their heads up and down every few seconds, to appease Rodney.

Actually, they were thinking about something else. They were thinking about their dead brother, Horace.

Part 2

Horace

A Weird Occurrence
at Horace's Funeral

When the two eccentric sisters' older brother Horace, who was also eccentric, died, a weird thing happened.

Everybody was standing around in the great room of the Morris mansion amid the placid, deathlike quietude of wreaths and flowers, murmuring vague condolences to one another about Horace's untimely demise, when suddenly out of nowhere came this strange noise.

It started as a low rumble, then became a harsh mechanical grinding.

Alter a few moments of startled confusion, somebody located the source of the sound.

"It's coming from Horace's study," said that person. "It's something going on inside Horace's safe!"

Horace's safe was a huge walk-in safe, and it was virtually impenetrable. It was an antique, even when he first got it (and that was a while back—his sisters were barely teenagers when Horace inherited it from his Uncle Allister, who was disposing of the assets of a failed bank). But no plans had yet been made for the opening of the safe, as no one had any idea how to go about getting into it. So all the bereaved people just stood there in Horace's study, listening to this awful grinding noise, totally bewildered.

This went on for about five minutes or so. Then it stopped.

What It Was Was

It took about a week to get into Horace's safe.* But they finally did it. And what they found when they pulled back the massive metal door was some sort of a curious machine, all riddled with belts and pulleys.

There was a wire running from the machine to what appeared to be a partially-disassembled alarm clock. And the floor of the safe was covered several inches deep in scraps of jagged paper.

What it was was the world's first paper shredder, which Horace had invented. And it had just ground all of Horace's documents into confetti.

* Because of disagreement among the relatives over the best way to go about getting into it

Trash

Horace's paper shredding contraption was examined by the people responsible for plundering through the possessions of dead people. Horace had built it out of a discarded corn husker. It was determined that he'd stored his documents in a bin which acted as a feeder into the paper shredder.

The partially-disassembled alarm clock was a timer mechanism, which had to be reset every 72 hours to prevent it from turning the thing on. After Horace had been dead for three days, the timer turned the thing on.

The shredded paper was gathered up and stuffed into boxes and saved for a while. Whatever it was that Horace didn't want anybody knowing about after he was dead was certainly not going to be known about now, unless somebody wanted to spend a lifetime or two putting all those little shreds of paper back together. So the boxes were eventually deemed worthless and set out on the street with the trash.

This Was The Moment

This was the moment Doris and Delores had been waiting for. They couldn't wait to get their hands on those boxes. So early the next morning, before dawn, one of them* went out and got the boxes and replaced them with empty boxes so no one would notice that the original boxes were missing.

They hid the boxes in a little round room up in one of the turrets of the mansion, which adjoined their bedroom.

That very afternoon, Doris and Delores got to work doing what would indeed end up taking two lifetimes to accomplish: putting back together Horace's documents, shred by shred.

* Delores

Not Guilty

Doris and Delores both felt a tinge of guilt over the stunt they pulled, as if they had pilfered something from the family under duplicitous conditions. But there was no need. You can't steal what is already yours. What they didn't know was, Horace had bequeathed all his documents to his sisters. His will was supposed to remain intact for whomever cracked his safe. Unfortunately, he had inadvertently left it in the feeding bin of the paper shredder and it, too, had been gnawed to shreds.

Rumors

The two eccentric sisters worked in secrecy for years, spending their days holed up in that turret finagling with little pieces of paper while their friends down below were living real lives: coming out as debutantes, traveling to Europe, courting potential spouses, etc.

Several rumors circulated around town about why hardly anyone ever saw those two Morris girls on Avocado Avenue. One was that they both were incestuous lesbian nymphomaniacs. Another was that they were actually triplets, and that the third one—who was supposed to have been named Lois—was either (a) grotesquely deformed, or (b) a lunatic.

(There was even a quadruplet version that was popular for a while—the fourth sister was supposed to be an incurable nudist—but it never quite caught on as much as the lunatic triplet theory.)

The two eccentric sisters, though, paid little heed to

the opinions of their peers. They were too engrossed in assembling this multi-thousand-piece jigsaw puzzle their brother had left behind.

I Always Come Back

The two eccentric sisters did not just throw away their prime years thoughtlessly, or out of mere curiosity. They had good reason: they were convinced that their brother had not actually died, but had become permanently invisible.

When they were children, Horace used to tell his sisters that he had figured out the secret of invisibility. At first they believed him, they were so young and impressionable. Then, as they grew older, they stopped believing him.

"How could we have been so gullible?" they used to laugh.

But Horace's invisibility tales were so persistent, and grew so convoluted, that they finally decided he must be telling the truth, so they started believing him again.

He could do it only for a few minutes at a time, he claimed. And while he was invisible, he couldn't speak or move things. And it always left him with a vague headache and a tingling in his fingertips for several hours, along with an indescribable feeling that he was more than one person. And for some strange reason, after each invisibility session, there was always a faint lingering scent of rutabagas.

He would never let them see him do it, and he never gave any indication of how he did it, although they were pretty sure mirrors were involved in some way.

Shortly before Horace vanished, he revealed to his sisters that he had been making headway in figuring out how to stay invisible for longer periods of time. This caused his sisters some consternation, but he was quick to assure them it was OK, that he always came back. In fact, those were the last words they ever heard their brother say.

"I always come back."

They Never Gave Up Hope

After Horace's untimely demise (or disappearance), the two eccentric sisters were surer than ever that he had been telling them the truth, and that he was not actually dead. After all, no body was ever found.

Of course, he could have since died. The two eccentric sisters were now pretty old, and Horace was even older, by seven years. It could well be that he had died invisible.

Or, he could have starved to death, since he was unable to manipulate objects while invisible. (Or, he could have suffocated, for that matter, if his lungs were unable to manipulate air.)

Or, the invisibility itself could have killed him.

And there was always the off chance that Horace "disappeared" for other reasons. Like gambling debts, or a run-in with a Mafioso, or an extended stint in the Witness Protection Program (like his cousin Thaddeus had had to do). This seemed unlikely, though, as Horace had never been known to associate with any unsavory characters (save for Thaddeus).

Which of these theories, if any, held a vestige of credibility the two eccentric sisters simply didn't know. But they never gave up hope that Horace was alive, perhaps living right there in the Morris mansion on Avocado Avenue.

And they were determined, no matter what it took, to reassemble Horace's documents. If he was still alive, they thought, there might be something in the documents that would tell them how to bring him back to a state of visibility, or at least how to communicate with him. Not to mention that they might discover for themselves the secret of invisibility, and perhaps, if they were lucky, even figure out how to put it into some kind of a salve.

Salve

The two eccentric sisters got along swimmingly, primarily because the sister who didn't say anything never disagreed with the sister who spoke.

Usually.

But in the matter of using Horace's life's work to turn in visibility into a salve, there was a disparity of opinion.

Doris thought it should be made into an unguent, but Dolores insisted it should be a balm. She would have settled for ointment, but Doris was terrified of the word "ointment" (due to a traumatic childhood incident).

After a couple of weeks of—not altercation, exactly… let's just say spirited debate—they were browsing through a *Ladies' Home Journal* when they spotted a mail order advertisement for a liniment that magically banished wrinkles. Immediately they turned toward each other. Neither uttered a word. They both knew what the other was thinking. Vanishing cream!

Unfathomable Wealth

If the two eccentric sisters were indeed successful at unearthing the secret of invisibility—especially if they could turn it into a salve—they would realize unfathomable wealth. "Doris and Delores' Amazing Vanishing Cream," or whatever they ended up calling it, would be desired by everyone on the planet who wanted to disappear. Magicians would clamor for it. The scofflaw and fugitive market would be staggering. Perhaps even the CIA would be interested (unless they simply seized the patent, then conveniently made Doris and Delores "disappear").

Wealth, however, was not their primary motivation. The accumulation of material goods had never held that much allure for them. Mostly they wanted to reconnect with Horace.

"If only we could see his face one last time," they always said. (Well, one of them said.)

Plus—and this was one of the biggest perks—they could walk into their neighbors' houses and eavesdrop on what the townsfolk had been saying about them all these years.

Their one indulgence might be to realize a lifelong dream of owning a shiny new Hudson automobile, like cousin Thaddeus used to drive (they were not aware that it was no longer manufactured).

The balance of their fortune would be invested in an aggressive investment portfolio, focusing on market sectors they thought held long-term growth potential, such as encyclopedias, TV antennas and typewriter ribbons.

The Turning Point

Eventually the two young eccentric sisters, all holed up in their turret hideaway day in and day out, ceased to be so young anymore. Their girlfriends had all found husbands and had babies and built fine homes for themselves.

Then one day the two eccentric sisters' mother died and they inherited the mansion. This was a turning point in their quest for invisibility. No longer were they confined to their tiny secret room up in the turret. Now they had the entire house to themselves. Instead of laying the shreds out on the floor, they began sticking them up on the walls. Spreading it out made it easier to match up the pieces, they discovered, and pretty soon they were wallpapering the entire mansion with it.

I'd Like to Rub Your Thigh

The two eccentric sisters did have one thing going for them: the paper shredder Horace had built was very crude, and it ground and chopped his documents into irregular shapes and sizes, which made the job of piecing them back together a little more tenable then would have been the case with a modern-day paper shredder. Still, though, it was a painstaking task, some what akin to putting together a gargantuan jigsaw puzzle without having any clue to what the picture is supposed to be.

But after a while, complete passages did begin to appear. They had nothing to do with invisibility, though. Some of it was Horace's pontifications about the universe, with smatterings of freeverse poetry reminiscent of the trancendentalists such as Whitman and Emerson, and occasional epistles about his passionate love of natural weather anomalies, in the tradition of John Muir. And much of it was simply a journal of the day-to-day occurrences of Horace's life.

There was also correspondence between Horace and various ladyfriends he was courting. In places it got rather torrid (by the two eccentric sisters' standards), as evidenced by this passage which materialized on the east wall of the sitting room, just above the mantle:

Your eyes are two of the fairest stars in all the heaven, yet the brightness of your cheek would shame those stars. O, how you lean your cheek upon your hand! O that I were a glove upon that hand, that I might touch that cheek.

I'd also like to rub your thigh. I mean, if you wouldn't mind or anything. Just along the outside part. OK?

You could always tell when Horace stopped copying stuff he found in books and started writing in his own inimitable style.

At first the two eccentric sisters were embarrassed by Horace's lusty correspondence, but after a while, they got used to living with all those tawdry phrases on their walls. It was a small price to pay if it meant getting any closer to being reunited with their long-lost brother, or figuring out how to make invisibility into a salve.

Horace and Horace

As Horace's fragmented musings materialized around them, Doris and Delores came to feel as if they were living in a giant diary. A diary not only of their brother's life but of their own. Their ever-evolving wallpaper triggered a plethora of childhood memories. Like Horace's encounter with ball lightning, and the time Horace surprised Doris with baby budgie, which she named Waldo, after Horace's childhood hero, Ralph Waldo Emerson.*

Some of these memories they began to look back on with a fresh perspective, reinterpreting them in a new light. The light of invisibility.

One such memory surfaced when Delores unfolded a gnarled shred of paper that made mention of a "bridle and saddle." It put her in mind of the incident with Horace's horse Horace. (The horse had already been named by its previous owners when Horace got him for his birthday.)

*Or so she thought. Actually it was Walt Whitman.

They awoke one morning to a commotion in the Morris household. Their parents had summoned the town constable. It seems that someone had absconded with Horace (the horse). The crime was never solved and has remained, to this day, shrouded in mystery. Oddly, the one family member who seemed the calmest through this ordeal was Horace.

What was curious was, Horace continued to spend a lot of time in the stable. He went out there every night after supper. And the stable floor stayed littered with bits of hay. And it still smelled like horse.

Then one August morning Delores was out for her biweekly beauty walk in the nude to replenish her skin with the morning dew.* She spotted what she thought was the form of a human figure across a long field, gliding through the mist several feet off the ground in a jerky bobbling motion. At the time, she wrote it off to some sort of illusion, like a heat inversion or a low-flying bird. Or perhaps a perceptual anomaly in her brain (she had recently gotten over a bout with the vapours). But now it all made sense: What other explanation could there be but that Horace, whether intentionally or by accident, had turned Horace invisible and was out for a ride?

*To put this in context, "nude," to Doris, meant nothing but pantaloons, stockings, a corset and a sundress.

Horace Appears

Doris never kept Waldo in a cage, he was a free range bird. He lived happily amongst the branches of a small plum tree she set up in the sitting room, free to light on the sisters' heads and shoulders and nuzzle their ears, or even nibble off Doris' dinner plate.

But freedom comes with risk, and one day a slight navigational miscalculation brought Waldo in contact with the blade of a slowly moving yet lethal ceiling fan.*

During Waldo's wake, through soft candlelight and teary eyes, Doris was startled to look up and see Horace. He was gazing at her from the adjacent room. His face had materialized between the words on the wall of what had been his study.

Delores saw it too, eventually, but only after doing a lot of squinting while Doris peeled an onion under her nose.

Doris was convinced it was an apparition. But the next morning Delores examined the wall at close range

*Actually it was Waldo III, but they still called him Waldo.

and discovered what was really going on. There were inconsistencies in Horace's handwriting. Whenever he dipped his pen in his inkwell, the ink would be denser and darker, growing gradually thinner and lighter as he wrote until he dipped again. Which was not very often—Horace wasn't a big dipper—so the variances were quite pronounced.

Once they became aware of these patterns, they couldn't unsee them. And their imaginings ran rampant. Oftentimes the images they thought they saw in the handwriting seemed to illustrate whatever Horace was writing about. Seascapes, mountain ranges, clouds, a duck. And occasionally, when their vision was compromised or their consciousness discombobulated—perhaps by the fatigue of a late-night puzzle-assembly session, or the ingestion of too much Ovaltine—a phantom image of Horace's face would appear.

As the two eccentric sisters resurrected their long lost brother's memoirs all around them, not only were they learning more about who he was, they increasingly sensed he was with them, watching them. In some ways, they felt as if they were getting to know him better in death—or in invisibility—than in life.

Paydirt

Finally, after years of laboriously reconstructing Horace's documents on the walls of the mansion, the two eccentric sisters had just this morning struck what they hoped was pay dirt: a direct reference to invisibility.

For all the curious comments Horace had made to his young sisters about how he could become invisible, he had never written anything specifically about invisibility. Not that they had found. They'd come upon the word "visibility" a few times, and got pretty excited about it each time, but it always turned out to be in reference to weather conditions. Then, just this morning, Delores picked up a random shred of paper from a box, a bigger shred than usual—it was gnarled and twisted, having apparently gotten hung up in the jaws of Horace's corn husker—and unfurled it to reveal the phrase "started to become invis."

Needless to say, this sent a jolt of excitement all the

way to their twenty toes. But before they went haywire, to be on the safe side, they scoured the unabridged dictionary in the sitting room to see if the word "invis" could possibly have any ending other than "ible." The only thing they found was an obscure fungus called *Corticium invisum,* but Horace would have no reason to be writing about that, as he had a deep-seated aversion to fungi. (This was related to the same incident that instilled in Doris a phobia about the word "ointment.") It looked like there was no other solution. This was it.

It was this exciting new development that had incited the two eccentric sisters to have a cup of Ovaltine. And it was this that they were thinking about as they sat on Sally's porch swing, bobbing their heads up and down so that Rodney would think they were listening to his incessant novel.

Part 3

Tea's Ready

Ballerina

Sally came out of the kitchen with five huge tumblers of iced tea on a tray, and a little sprig of mint in each tumbler, which she'd just pulled fresh out of the garden. She walked slowly and deliberately, like a ballerina.

On the way to the front porch, she stopped by the parlor where the old man was sitting.

"Don't you want to come back out on the porch now?' she said. The old man said what he always said when the two eccentric sisters were there (which Sally knew full well he'd say):

"I do not intend to sit out on any porch with two incestuous lesbian nymphomaniacs."

Sally rolled her eyes and walked over to the old man so he could take his tumbler of tea off the tray. Then, as always, she let out a little sigh, to signify that she didn't approve of his attitude.

The old man paid no heed, he just sipped his tea.

On The Porch

Sally stepped out onto the porch with the tray of tea. Each eccentric sister took one, and Rodney took one. Then Sally sat back down in her big white rocking chair.

"Rodney is favoring us with a reading from his novel," said one of the eccentric sisters.

"Oh?" said Sally.

"Well, actually it's more of a novella," said Rodney. "I guess I should have waited till you came back out before I started reading it. Would j'all like me to start over?"

The two eccentric sisters did not want Rodney to start over, so one of them, the one who does all the talking, decided to recap Sally on what had happened so far in Rodney's novella, based on the scant bits of it that had accidentally leaked through to her consciousness while she'd been bobbing her head and thinking about her brother's alleged invisibility.

"It seems that these people are somewhere looking for something," she explained.

Sally waited for the eccentric sister to go on, but that was all she had to say. So Sally turned to Rodney, assuming he'd want to elaborate. But he just shrugged.

"That's about it," he said.

Ice Cubes

The ice cubes made little clacking sounds against the sides of the plastic tumblers whenever Sally or an eccentric sister took a sip of tea.

This, along with the chattering of sparrows, plus an occasional echo of a dog barking or a child laughing, provided a quiet soundtrack for the continuation of Rodney's novella.

Potato Salad

As Rodney began droning again, the two eccentric sisters put their heads on automatic bob and went back to thinking about Horace.

Is he still alive?

Is there any way he can be rematerialized, or communicated with?

Can invisibility be made into a salve?

Etc.

And Sally lapsed into a reverie about a man she saw in the drug store the other day. He was having a sundae at the soda fountain while waiting to get a prescription filled, and he flirted with her a little, causing her to knock over a display of flip flops. Right now in her reverie, they were picnicking beside a babbling brook, eating potato salad.

The only real babbling going on, however, was Rodney's. He was still rattling on about some people somewhere looking for something, thinking everybody on the porch was hanging on to his every word.

Rodney Finally Said It

While Rodney read, a small airplane passed by overhead. The soothing mellow drone of its single engine, fading slowly into the distance, blended with Rodney's own droning to produce a gentle hum that no one the porch paid the least bit of attention to.

Then Rodney read something that changed all that. "And there it stood, in the clearing," he read. "Out in a vast, grassy meadow atop a hill. Its shape appeared to be oddly gazeboesque."

At the word "gazeboesque" both the eccentric sisters looked up, their thoughts of Horace vanishing like bubbles popping.

"As the people drew nearer, they could clearly see that it was indeed a gazebo," read Rodney. "A gazebo in the middle of nowhere."

At this, the two eccentric sisters began poking each other with their elbows and cackling like two giddy hens. They had long given up on ever hearing Rodney say "a gazebo in the middle of nowhere" again, and they were taken completely by surprise. The eccentric sister who never says anything even began slapping her knees and pattering her feet on the floor of the porch, creating a terrible commotion. It was the most noise anyone had ever heard her make, and it startled Sally out of her potato salad reverie.

Rodney couldn't understand what everybody found so amusing all of a sudden, but he was delighted that somebody was at last showing some response to his novella.

The Old Man

"What's going on out there?" came a voice from inside the house. (It was the old man's.)

"He said it!" called the eccentric spokesister for the two eccentric sisters. "Rodney said it! He said, 'A gazebo in the middle of nowhere'! We heard him!"

Needless to say, the old man wasn't nearly as amused by all this as were the two eccentric sisters, who were downright ecstatic.

"Lame-brained nymphos," he mumbled to himself, shaking his head.

NBC'll

"That's as much as I've written so far," said Rodney.

"Oh, it was charming!" said the eccentric spokesister. "Positively charming! We especially enjoyed the part about the gazebo."

Actually, of course, that was about as much of it as she had heard.

"I'm going to try to sell it to NBC as a mini-series," said Rodney. "I think NBC'll buy it."

"Oh, that would be lovely," said the eccentric sister, having no idea what he was talking about, as neither of the two eccentric sisters watched, or even owned, a television.

Jigsaw Puzzle

The two eccentric sisters, having finished their tumblers of tea, and having at last fulfilled their dream of hearing Rodney say "a gazebo in the middle of nowhere," stood up.

"Are you leaving?" said Sally, looking somewhat befuddled.

This was not their regularly scheduled time to stand up.

"Yes, we have to get back early today," explained the eccentric spokessister. "We have things to do."

"You know, I won a jigsaw puzzle at the bake-off. It was for my caramel okra. It's huge, like a trajillion pieces. I was thinking we could dump it out on the dining room table and start trying to put it together, if y'all'd be interested."

The two eccentric sisters didn't say anything.

"It might be a relaxing way to end a Sunday afternoon," Sally continued. "You know, something different."

"Thank you, no," said one sister as the other one shook her head in big, slow swoops like the old man watching a ping pong match.

Usually the two sisters consulted with each other with a brief glance before making a collective decision, such as accepting an invitation, but faced with the specter of spending their cherished off-time putting together a giant jigsaw puzzle, no consultation was required.

Bye Now

The two eccentric sisters walked down the brick walkway and opened the little wooden gate.

"Bye now," said Sally.

"Bye" said the eccentric spokesister. Then she nodded her head slightly.

She always did that when she was leaving.

She was predictable that way.

The sisters stepped onto the walkway and sauntered back down the sidewalk toward the mansion, all wallpapered with memories and musings and tawdry plagiarizations, to return to their real-life jigsaw puzzle and resume their lifelong task of reuniting with their brother. And perhaps inventing an invisibility salve.

Mrs. Whitmore

Across the street, Mrs. Whitmore was peering through the curtains.

"There go two of those Morris triplets, back to that mansion to tend to their maniac sister," she muttered to her husband, who was watching a baseball game.

"She ain't no maniac, Ethyl, she's a nudist," he muttered back.

Their tone was that crotchety, yammery cadence of having been married 42 years.

"Incurable!" he added, his eyes never leaving the game.

Rodney

Rodney, fired with renewed determination, dashed inside and ran up to his room to get back to work writing his novella, which, after such a rousing reaction from the two eccentric sisters, he'd decided to call—what else?—*A Gazebo in the Middle of Nowhere.*

"NBC'll buy this for sure," he said out loud as he wrote.

The Old Man

Sally went into the parlor to tell the old man it was safe to come out, now that the two eccentric sisters had gone home, but he had fallen asleep.

Sally

Sally spent the balance of the afternoon in the garden, digging the weeds. The light was getting low, but she figured she had a good hour.

The Sisters

On the porch, the rocking chairs stood silent now. The sparrows were gone, too. In the front yard a cricket started chirping, followed by another, then another.

Eventually dusk fell. One by one, lights blinked on in the houses up and down the street. The bulky silhouette of the Morris mansion, though, stood in darkness, save for one tiny upstairs window, through which could be seen the shadows of what appeared to be three human forms, flickering against the wall in soft candlelight.

Except for the chirping of the crickets, which had melded now into a gentle din, everything was quiet on Avocado Avenue.

Reconstruct Horace's last will and testament at

PilliardDickle.com/Horace

www.ingramcontent.com/pod-product-compliance
Lightning Source LLC
Chambersburg PA
CBHW052358060726
47592CB00019B/1529